Angelina's Pet

GROSSET & DUNLAP
Penguin Young Readers Group
An Imprint of Penguin Random House LLC

Published by Grosset & Dunlap, an imprint of Penguin Random House LLC, 345 Hudson Street, New York, New York 10014.
GROSSET & DUNLAP is a trademark of Penguin Random House LLC. Manufactured in China.

ISBN 978-0-448-48742-7 10 9 8 7 6 5 4 3 2 1

Angelina's Pet

Inspired by the classic children's book series
by author Katharine Holabird and illustrator Helen Craig

Grosset & Dunlap
An Imprint of Penguin Random House

It is a beautiful spring day in Chipping Cheddar. Angelina Ballerina and her best friend, Alice, are walking home from ballet class.

“Look at the pretty bird, Alice!” Angelina exclaims. “He flies so gracefully! I wish I could have a bird of my own as a pet.”

“Just imagine how much fun it would be to dance with him! He could fly around you as you twirl and leap!” Alice says.

Angelina rushes home to tell her mom her big idea.

"Mom, I just saw the most gorgeous bird in the park. He would make an excellent pet. Can I *please* get a pet of my own?" Angelina begs.

"Angelina, having a pet is a lot of responsibility, but I think you are ready for it. Why don't you think about what kind of pet you would like to have," Mrs. Mouseling says.

"Yippee!" Angelina shouts.

Hmmm . . . What kind of pet would be the most fun to play with? Angelina wonders. *Mrs. Tippytoes has lots of animals at her house! I will go visit her to get some ideas.*

At Mrs. Tippytoes's house, Angelina dances with a bird,

holds a ladybug,

and strokes a caterpillar.

She can't decide what kind of pet she wants!

Just then, Angelina sees a beautiful butterfly fluttering around Mrs. Tippytoes's garden.

"I did a dance at ballet school called the Butterfly Dance. I love butterflies!" Angelina cries.

“Can I borrow your butterfly, Mrs. Tippytoes? I will take good care of her,” Angelina says.

“Of course you can, Angelina,” says Mrs. Tippytoes. “Butterflies love to fly around visiting all the flowers, so keep a close eye on her.”

Angelina scoops up the butterfly and begins to walk home.

Angelina is having a wonderful time following the butterfly. On the way home, they stop at different flowers, smelling each one as they go.

But suddenly the butterfly flutters away.

"Come here, butterfly! Fly back to my hand. Let's go visit Alice! She will be so happy to meet you!" Angelina shouts.

But the butterfly flutters farther and farther away.

Angelina runs after her butterfly. The butterfly stops at a garden right in front of her ballet school.

"Miss Lilly, can you help me catch my pet butterfly?" Angelina asks.

Miss Lilly leaps in the air, but the butterfly flies even higher.

The butterfly continues to flutter along through Chipping Cheddar until she reaches Alice's garden.

Alice is busy in the kitchen with her mom sewing a new ballet costume.

"Alice, can you help catch my pet butterfly?" Angelina calls out to her friend.

Alice and Miss Lilly both chase after the butterfly. Suddenly, Angelina has an idea. She sees a net in Alice's garage. It's the perfect thing to catch her butterfly!

Swoosh! Angelina catches the butterfly in the net and takes her safely back to Mrs. Tippytoes.

Mrs. Mouseling is waiting for Angelina when she comes home.

“I’m not sure I’m ready to take care of a pet on my own yet,” Angelina says sadly as she begins to tell her mom all about her afternoon.

Mrs. Mouseling gives Angelina a big hug. “Yes, you are! When you were in trouble, you knew to ask your friends for help,” she says with a smile.

A few days later, Mrs. Mouseling arrives home with a special surprise for Angelina.

“Angelina, I want you to meet your new pet. I know you will take great care of her,” Mrs. Mouseling says.

Angelina jumps up and down and *pirouettes* around the room. "Thanks so much, Mom! I can't believe it—a fish of my very own! I am going to name her Plié. I can't wait to show Alice and all of my friends at ballet school. They will all want to help me take care of her—and I'm going to make sure I ask for their help when I need it. This is the best surprise ever!" she says, hugging the fishbowl tight.